JUST THE WAY YOU ARE

Marcus Pfister

Translated by **Marianne Martens**

NORTH-SOUTH BOOKS

NEW YORK ✳ LONDON

"Hello, Lion," said Hedgehog. "Are you coming to the party tonight?"

"Oh, no one cares whether I come or not," said Lion sadly. "If only I had a beak and wings like Toucan, then everyone would admire me."

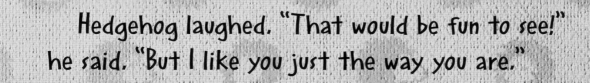

Hedgehog laughed. "That would be fun to see!" he said. "But I like you just the way you are."

"Hello, Hedgehog," said Toucan. "Are you coming to the party tonight?"

Hedgehog thought about what Lion had said. "Oh, no one cares if I come or not," he said sadly. "If only I were as bright and shiny as you or Chameleon, then everyone would admire me."

Toucan laughed. "That would be fun to see!"
he said. "But I like you just the way you are."

"Hello, Toucan," said Chameleon. "Are you coming to the party tonight?"

Toucan thought about what Hedgehog had said. "Oh, no one cares if I come or not," he said sadly. "If only I were as big and strong as Elephant, then everyone would admire me."

"Hello, Chameleon," said Elephant. "Are you coming to the party tonight?"

Chameleon thought about what Toucan had said. "Oh, no one cares if I come or not," he said sadly. "If only I were as elegant as Stork, then everyone would admire me."

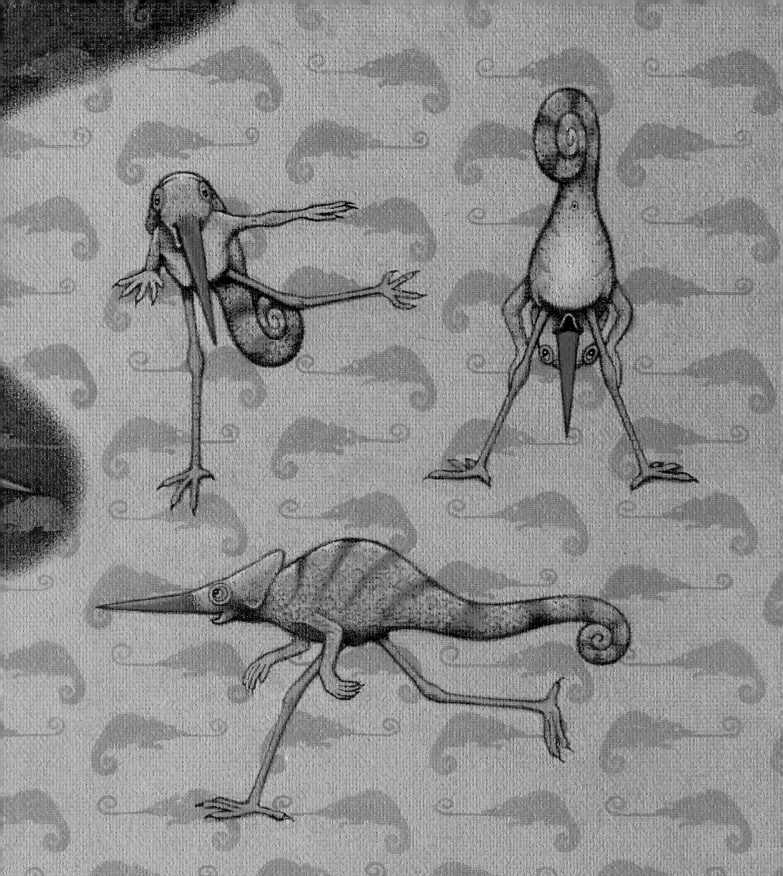

Elephant laughed. "That would be fun to see!"
he said. "But I like you just the way you are."

"Hello, Elephant," said Stork. "Are you coming to the party tonight?"

Elephant thought about what Chameleon had said. "Oh, no one cares if I come or not," he said sadly. "If only I could hop like Kangaroo, then everyone would admire me."

Stork laughed. "That would be fun to see!" he said. "But I like you just the way you are."

"Hello, Stork," said Kangaroo. "Are you coming to the party tonight?"

Stork thought about what Elephant had said. "Oh, no one cares if I come or not," he said sadly. "If only I had a mane like Lion, then everyone would admire me."

Kangaroo laughed. "That would be fun to see!" he said. "But I like you just the way you are."

That evening, everyone
came to the party after all.
When Kangaroo told how
Stork had wished for a mane
like Lion, Lion felt very proud.
Stork liked his mane!
Then all the animals told each
other what they had wished for.
Each animal was proud that one of his friends had
admired something about him. And they all laughed
and laughed as they imagined how they would have
looked if their wishes had come true.
It was a wonderful party filled with good times
and good friends.